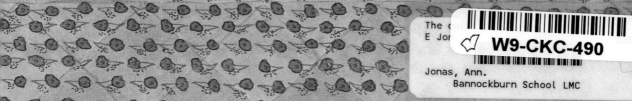
E
Jon   Jonas, Ann
The Quilt

DATE DUE

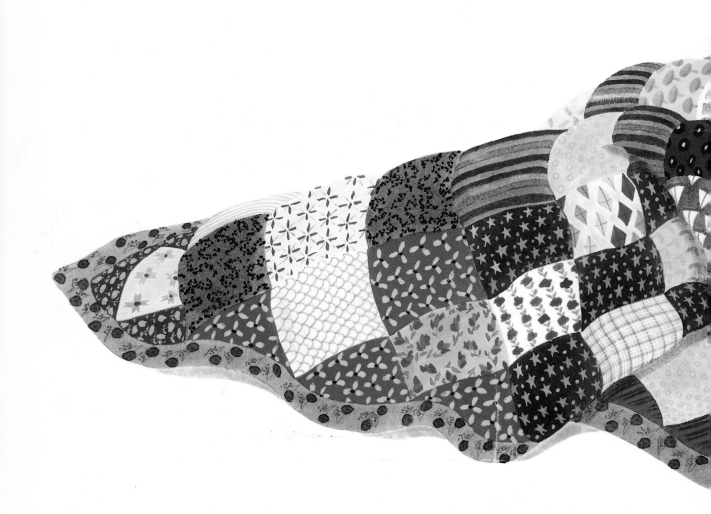

For Nina

Library of Congress Cataloging
in Publication Data
Jonas, Ann. The quilt.
Summary: A child's new patch-
work quilt recalls old memories and
provides new adventures at bedtime.
[1. Quilts—Fiction.
2. Bedtime—Fiction] I. Title.
PZ7.J664Qi 1984   [E]   83-25385
ISBN 0-688-03825-5
ISBN 0-688-03826-3 (lib. bdg.)

The Quilt
Ann Jonas
Greenwillow Books/New York

I have a new quilt.

It's to go on my new grown-up bed.

My mother and father
made it for me. They used
some of my old things.
Here are my first curtains
and my crib sheet. Sally
is lying on my baby pajamas.

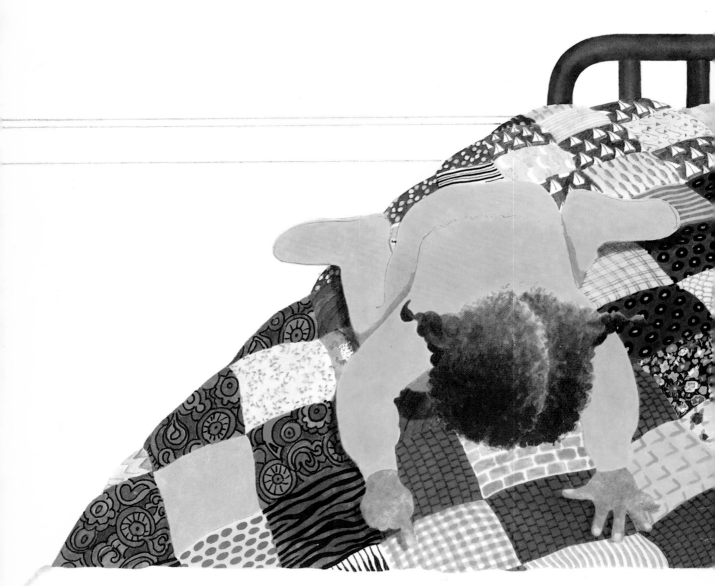

That's the shirt I wore on
my second birthday.
This piece is from my
favorite pants. They got
too small. The cloth my
mother used to make Sally
is here somewhere.
I can't find it now.

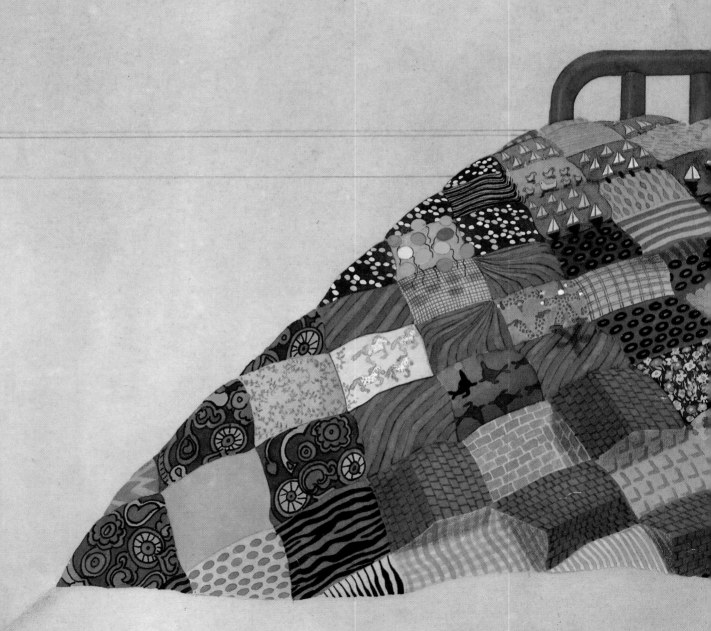

I know I won't be able
to go to sleep tonight.

It almost looks
like a little town....

I can't find Sally!

Maybe she's here.
Sally!

She wouldn't like it here.
Sally!

If she hid here,
I'd never find her.
Sally!

She wouldn't be here.
She doesn't like water.
Sally!

This is worse than the tunnel!
Sally!

I see her!

Good
morning,
Sally.

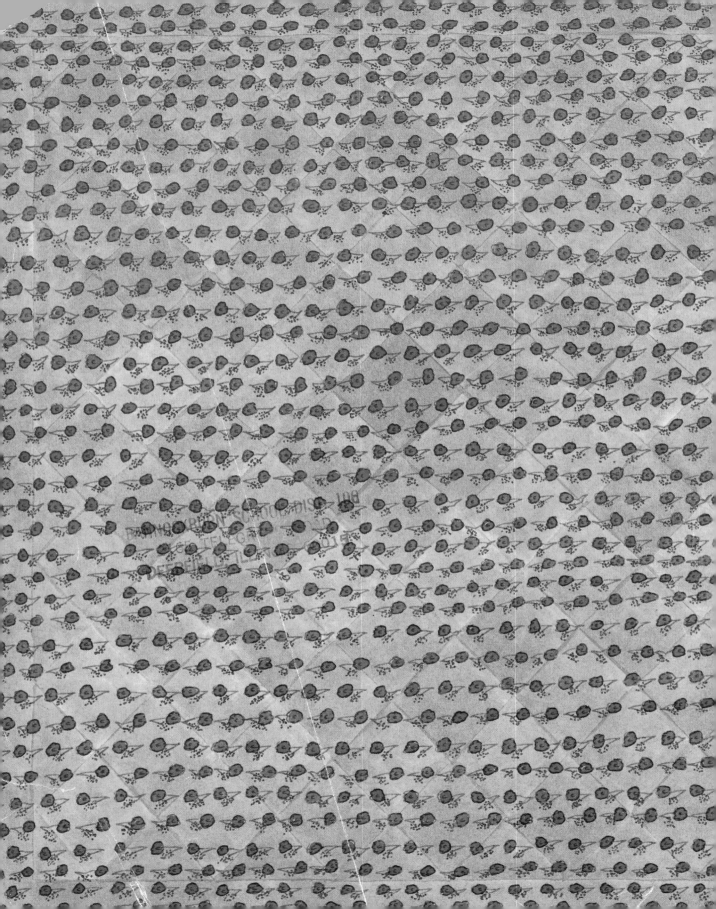